Renegade Ornaments

Heidi Wolfe

Illustrated by
Dabby Oppenheimer

AuthorHouse™
1663 Liberty Drive
Bloomington, IN 47403
www.authorhouse.com
Phone: 833-262-8899

Because of the dynamic nature of the Internet, any web addresses or links contained in this book may have changed since publication and may no longer be valid. The views expressed in this work are solely those of the author and do not necessarily reflect the views of the publisher, and the publisher hereby disclaims any responsibility for them.

Any people depicted in stock imagery provided by Getty Images are models, and such images are being used for illustrative purposes only.
Certain stock imagery © Getty Images.

Interior Image Credit: Dabby Oppenheimer

This book is printed on acid-free paper.

ISBN: 978-1-6655-4241-8 (sc)
ISBN: 978-1-6655-4240-1 (hc)
ISBN: 978-1-6655-4242-5 (e)

Library of Congress Control Number: 2021921861

Print information available on the last page.

Published by AuthorHouse 10/28/2021

This book is dedicated to
Dabby Oppenheimer
who is the illustrator, mother
and best friend of this book's Author.

'Twas the week before Christmas, and in the front room of the Williams' house, right in front of a beautiful bay window, sat a spectacular Christmas tree. It glittered with ornaments of shapes and sizes. At the top, the most beautiful angel perched high above all of the ornaments. She wore a silk gown trimmed in lace and threads of gold. Her shimmering hair seemed to pick up the shades of the sparkling lights strung about the tree.

The angel was very proud of her place on the tree, as if she were in charge and had a bird's eye view of all the activities going on around the tree. At times, if you looked very carefully, you could see her gaze down over the other ornaments to be sure they knew she was there watching over them.

Down at the very bottom of the tree, near the floor, hung two ornaments. One was silver and other was red. The silver ornament glanced up at the angel with a sneer on his face.

"You know, she is always up there," said the silver ornament. The red one smiled, and said, "Yep. Year after year. She looks good up there, too. Makes the whole tree look special."

"How come she gets to represent us?" The silver ornament complained, feeling quite cranky and out of sorts. "I mean, don't you think that...well, maybe..."

"Don't say it!" the red ornament said. "Remember last year when you thought it would be fun to jump off the tree and hide until Easter so we could see the other holidays, too? We had to sit in those bushes until someone found us and put us back in the boxes marked 'Christmas'."

The silver ornament screwed up his face in thought.

"Oh, no, you have that look..." worried the red ornament.

"Why can't you and I have the top spot this year?" Silver said. "I mean, we have been on this tree for years, and I think we deserve it. She won't mind."

"Not much!" said Red. "She won't let us up there."

"You forget you're with me. I'll get you there!"

"Okay, so we agree we should sit on top," Red said. "How are we gonna get there?" He couldn't believe he'd even considered it.

The two of them hung there for a while thinking of a plan. They were so naïve.

"I know," said Silver confidently. "We'll jump from the branch to branch. Easy!"

The silver ornament started first. He swayed back and forth and jumped up and down until his branch launched him up to the next branch. Luck followed him, he managed to grab another branch and was elevated to the next level. "Come on up, the weather's fine," he yelled to Red.

Red tried to do the same, but just ended up getting more and more tired. "I can't do it," he panted.

"Nonsense. Just try harder. You want the top, don't you?"
"Yes, but I..."
"Then swing for all you're worth," Silver encouraged.

So the red ornament began to sway and bounce, up and down,
harder and harder, until without his even noticing it, he'd reached
the branch above, and kept on bouncing.

"You can rest now, you've made it to the next one," said Silver.

"I did?" Red asked, pleased with himself.

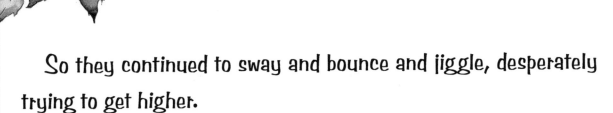

So they continued to sway and bounce and jiggle, desperately trying to get higher.

Things were going rather well until—

"Ahhhhhhhhhhh!" yelled Silver. He'd swayed too hard and ended up in the back of Jimmy's fire truck on the floor.

"Good move there, Slick," yodeled Red.

"I just got overly excited, that's all. I'll be right there," Silver exclaimed.

Well, that sounded easy enough, but Silver found he was stuck!

"King of the mountain! I'm gonna get there first!" Red yelled. And he started to climb harder. He bounced and wiggled and traveled quite nicely, considering all the pressure he was under.

Just then the little boy named Jimmy came into the room and sat down to his fire truck. He reached into the back where Engineer Bob should sit. "Hey, you're not Engineer Bob," he said. "What are you doing in my truck? I better put you back on the tree before you break."

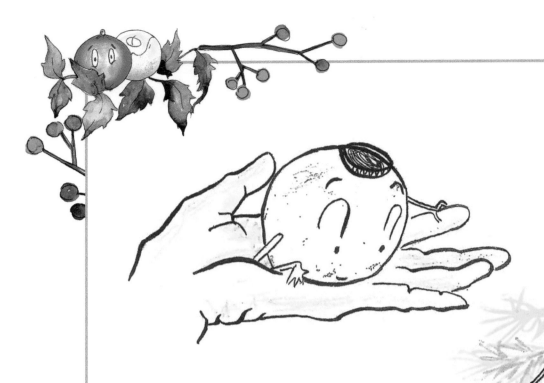

Slowly Jimmy lifted Silver up as if he were an elevator, passing Red who was struggling with all his might, and stuck him on the tree—higher than where Red sat.

"There, you look nice where you belong," he said.

"That's what he thinks," Silver said. "I'm moving up. Hey, Red, did you miss me?"

With an exhausted look on his face, Red joined Silver's attempts to capture the top of the tree. As they bounced and bobbled and jiggled, at times they'd toss other ornaments off or knock them to a lower branch.

It really was not a pretty sight with blue, green, pink ornaments flying off in all directions, banging into walls and landing on lamp shades. Some managed to cling desperately to the curtains, while others flew across the living room to destinations no ornament should ever know.

"Sorry about that," Red and Silver would shout together.

The silver ornament always seemed to be getting into trouble. Granted, he was the trouble maker and often deserved it, yet somehow it just didn't seem fair to him. Moving up into position and feeling very smug, he attempted to reach for a branch that was a tiny bit out of his way, and SPLAT! He landed on the extra thick carpet. "Here we go again," he moaned. But then a look of sheer terror came over his face. The family cat spotted him!

"Curl up like a ball!" Red shouted from high up in the tree.

"I am a ball, you idiot!" Silver screamed as the cat, thinking Silver was a plaything, began bopping him about the house. Into furniture and around pillows, through doorways and down the steps into the den. The cat was having a marvelous time. Silver was getting a headache. If you were very quiet, you could hear the other ornaments laughing.

Finally, the silver ornament, who was not having a good day, sat motionless at the base of the stairs when he heard a terrible loud noise. It was the vacuum, and it was headed his way!

"You don't belong down here," a voice suddenly said, and Silver felt warm hand under him as the lady of the house stopped her cleaning to pick him up.

"You belong on the tree, not where you might get stepped on," and she proceeded to place him back on the tree.

Again the two ornaments struggled to climb higher, making the tree sway to and fro. From atop the tree, the angel looked down at them. "Excuse me," she said as she hung on for dear life. "Why are you bouncing up and down so much? You are throwing me off balance, and I fear I may fall."

"Well, it's like this. I think I should be on top of the tree this year. It only seems fair because you are always up there. I am a cool looking silver dude, and I think I would do the tree justice," Silver stated most eloquently.

"Hold it right there. What do you mean it is your turn? I thought we were both gonna get up there—together," said Red. "What makes you so special?" After all, he'd worked so hard to get there, he wasn't about to just hang by as Silver took the glory.

The two ornaments began to toss each other about, hoping to remove the other so they could get to the top. The angel held on as long as she could, but her small delicate hands just couldn't hold any longer and she flew off the tree onto the couch.

"Well, I never!" said the upside down, topsy-turvy angel. Her hair was all over her face, and her dress was wrapped about her in complete disarray.

Suddenly the two ornaments realized there was no angel at the top of the tree. They stopped their fighting and began to race to the top. Faster and faster they sprang. TWANG and BOUNCE and then

—they were both hanging on the top of the tree. **THE** place they both wanted to be. Both had a big smile on their face when...

In walked Liz, the little boy's sister, who plunked down on the couch to read a magazine, completely unaware that the ornaments were rebelling.

The angel tried to compose herself, and moved closer to the girl so she would notice and put her back on the tree. No such luck. The angel got more and more agitated, and began to flap her wings, harder and harder, trying to get Liz' attention.

Feeling something odd going on, Liz turned to look at the angel—

"Oh, no! After all of our work, she's coming back," Silver gasped. "Be very still so maybe they won't notice us up here."

Fat chance.

Liz frowned. "What are you two ornaments doing up here? You belong down lower.

The angel belongs up here. I guess I just have to move you down a little and put the angel where she should be," who suddenly lay as motionless statue. She'd achieve her goal. Liz packed up the beautiful but frazzled angel, and patted her dress and hair into place. "Why are you here and not on the tree?" she wondered. "I guess someone forgot to put you up on top. I better put you back before someone sits on you."

As Liz walked toward the tree holding the angel, you could see the look of triumph on the angel's face as she was about to reclaim her position atop the tree.

Liz said as she moved the red and silver ornaments to the bottom of the tree and carefully set the angel back on top.

The angel looked down at Silver and Red, and smiled. Then she quietly said, "Did someone use the term King of the Mountain? I like that. I like that a lot." And she folded her arms and grinned like she had never grinned before.

"Well," said Red, "at least here we are closer to the presents, and we can see the looks on the children's faces when they open their gifts on Christmas. Anyway, I'm tired."

Glancing up at the angel, Silver muttered, "Next year. Just wait."

The entire family and the ornaments had a wonderful Christmas. Red was right about enjoying the children, especially when the baby crawled up and saw his reflection in Red's shiny face. Silver thought about next year, but only when he wasn't enjoying the day, too. As for the other ornaments, well, they will need a whole year to recuperate.

So remember, sometimes being just where you are is the best gift of all.

CPSIA information can be obtained
at www.ICGtesting.com
Printed in the USA
BVHW020841161121
PP12842100001B/5

9 781665 542401